Elijah

Journey Throughout The year

JOANA JEHU-APPIAH

DEDICATION

To my sisters (Sarie, Marie and Deborah); I am blessed to have you in my life and honoured to be an aunty to your unique and wonderful children. Thank you for always believing in me.

To the SISTERHOOD (Tracey, Natasha, Sabrina, Chinma, Hannah and Lina); specifically, the mother's within this friendship group, what funny, boisterous and smart children you have raised. You are all incredible women.

To my God-children - Inaiya and Kaiden, and the many children, I am fortunate enough to call nieces and nephews, Zahara, Zakiah.. the list goes on. Thank you.

To my parents (Cynthia and Jerisdan), your faith and values have made me the person I am today.

Thank you Adeola Ogundele for inspiring me to publish my books.

... And lastly, to my dearest nephew Elijah, thank you for lending me your name.

Elijah rests on daddy,

Discussing the past year.

So many thoughts run through his mind;

He wants his daddy near.

Elijah's school closed mid-March,

And he was much confused,

Something was stirring across the world,

He watched it on the news.

Slowly it came; a virus,

Corona was its name,

Quite like an invisible monster,

So desperate for fame.

Itt started as an outbreak,

Then spread to overseas,

The government said:

'*You must stay home!*'

Now everything must cease.

Soon all the shelves were empty,

Nothing was guaranteed,

Mummy and daddy could not believe

The level of their greed.

And then it came; the lockdown

Because the virus spread,

The PM put this measure in place,

But doctors worked instead.

Daddy was put on furlough,

His business had to close.

Mummy and Daddy worked as a team,

But sometimes tempers rose.

Walks in the park were needed,

For exercise and air,

As everyone was a stranger there,

They practised thought and care.

Elijah drew a rainbow,

To thank the NHS,

Every Thursday they clapped and cheered,

It was a huge success.

Elijah grabs his face mask,

When heading into town,

Elijah is sure to put it on,

When people are around.

Elijah washes his hands,

To keep them nice and clean,

Twenty seconds is all that it takes,

It's now become routine.

Elijah joins a long queue,

To get into the stores.

Elijah stands two metres apart,

As foot prints mark the floor.

Elijah missed his grandma,

He missed his grandpa too,

FaceTime had been a whole lot of fun.

It helped them to get through.

Elijah had his birthday.

Elijah just turned six.

He blew his candles; he made a wish,

Hoping the world gets fixed.

Two men in America,

Just could not get along,

So much money so little respect,

As stations drew a throng.

The talk then turned to Brexit,

The UK sealed a deal,

The best way to live, work, buy and sell,

It was quite the ordeal.

And now there is a vaccine,

With so many now sick,

Invisible monster; *poof* be gone!

With just a jab, one prick.

'What's that you keep on reading?'

'It's called a journal son.

Your mother and I want to be sure,

So research must be done.'

'So will you take the vaccine?'

'As soon as we know enough,

Our only concern in all of this

Is for the ones we love.'

'It's time for bed Elijah;

It's time to sleep, my boy.

We pray better days in the New Year,

No tiers; just tears of joy.'

GLOSSARY OF TERMS

Asymptomatic   An infected person that does not show any symptoms, such as coughing or fever.

Covid 19   An infectious disease. 'CO' = Corona; 'VI' = Virus; 'D' = Disease; 2019 = year of outbreak. The name given to <u>SARS-CoV-2</u> by <u>the WHO</u> on 11 February 2020.

Epidemic (outbreak) A sudden outbreak of a disease within a community or region.

Face covering (Mask) Surgical/medical face masks are designed to be worn in medical settings and must meet regulatory <u>PPE</u> standards. Face coverings are designed to cover the nose and mouth safely; examples include a scarf or a bandana (face coverings do not need to meet PPE standards). Some people also choose to wear additional protective equipments such as a **Face visor** or a **shield.**

Flattening the curve   To spread out the rate of infection. The national health service (NHS) is best able to deal with patients over a long period of time than all at once.

Furlough   A UK government scheme that pays employees up to 80% of their salary, whilst they are on leave from work (due to the <u>coronavirus</u> <u>pandemic.</u>)

Herd Immunity The protection given to the population (of the UK) against the <u>coronavrius disease</u> due to high number of the people being <u>vaccinated.</u>

Immunization: A process that protects a person from a disease through <u>vaccination.</u>

(Self) Isolation   The act of separating an infected person from others. The infected person must stay at home away from others.

Key worker A job role that is considered to be crucial; provides an essential service, examples include: shop assistants, teachers, journalists and police officers. These individuals are often exempt from <u>lockdown</u> measures.

Lockdown A government measure that restricts the movement of people, and requires them to 'stay at home,' to stop the virus from spreading.

New Variant/Strain of the Virus Viruses mutate (make new copies of themselves.) These mutations are called variants. The new variant (discovered in the UK in late 2020) spreads more easily between people, increasing the R Number.

Pandemic An epidemic that has spread worldwide.

PPE (Personal protective equipment) Protective wear that is designed to protect a person from harm or infection, this could include wearing a face mask or a glove.

Pre-existing condition A medical illness that a person had before the coronavirus pandemic that makes them more vulnerable to the disease.

Quarantine To separate a person (that might have been exposed to the virus and does not know it yet or is asymptomatic) from others. The person's movement is restricted usually between 10 to 14 days to see if they have caught the disease. For example, a person that has travelled abroad might be asked to quarantine.

Remote/online learning The shift from classroom teaching to online teaching, connecting individuals by technology (computers).

R Number Reproduction number. The average number of people that an infected person will pass the disease on to.

SARS-CoV-2 Severe Acute Respiratory Syndrome Coronavirus 2. The virus responsible for COVID-19. Viruses often lead to diseases. SARS-CoV-2 was renamed as COVID 19 by the WHO.

Shielding Those who have been identified as clinically extremely vulnerable (at very high risk of severe illness from the coronavirus disease) advised to stay at home.

Social Distance To reduce social interaction between people. This includes keeping a distance of 2 metres apart from others (when in public).

Support Bubble A support network which links 2 households.

Tiers A system introduced by the government. Alert levels indicate the level of restrictions needed in a particular area. Tier 1 (Medium Alert) Tier 2 (High Alert) Tier 3 (Very High Alert) Tier 4 (Stay at home)

Transmission To transfer something (the virus) from one spot to another.

Unprecedented Never seen before, an incident that occurs for the very first time.

Vaccination A substance 'medicine' that is injected into the body to help protect against the <u>coronavirus</u> disease, to produce <u>immunity</u> to a specific disease.

The WHO The World Health Organization (WHO)

Working from Home (WFH) A policy that allows an employee to work from their home rather than at work.

A Second World War veteran,

*Called **Captain Sir Tom Moore***

Walked a hundred laps in his garden

Elijah was in awe.

For accuracy, definitions have been matched against the WHO and official UK Government website.

www.ingramcontent.com/pod-product-compliance
Lightning Source LLC
Chambersburg PA
CBHW041000170626
46815CB00002B/89